The FORGOTTEN FOREST of Oz

written and illustrated by

ERIC SHANOWER

Founded on and continuing
the famous Oz stories of L. Frank Baum.

FIRST PUBLISHING
TM & © 1988 FIRST PUBLISHING, INC.

For David.

Published by First Publishing, Inc.
435 N. LaSalle Street, Chicago IL 60610

ISBN: 0-915419-44-0

First Printing: October, 1988
1 2 3 4 5 6 7 8 9 0

Printed in the United States of America

Rick Obadiah, Publisher   Rick Oliver, Editor
Kathy Kotsivas, Operations Director   Larry Doyle, Managing Editor
Kurt Goldzung, Sales Director   Alex Wald, Art Director
Rich Markow, Traffic Manager   Mike McCormick, Production Manager

CROSS THE DEADLY DESERT FROM THE LAND OF OZ LIES THE FOREST OF **BURZEE**. IN THIS ANCIENT FOREST THE TRUNKS GROW TALL, THICK, AND STURDY, NEVER KNOWING THE SHARP CHOP OF AN AXE. TREE LIMBS SPRING FORTH MIGHTILY, BRANCHING AGAIN AND AGAIN TO FORM A LEAFY ROOF OVER THE TWILIGHT WORLD.

IF YOU WERE TO STAND IN THE FOREST OF BURZEE, STAND AS STILL AND AS QUIET AS THE GREAT TREES THEMSELVES, YOU WOULD BEGIN TO **HEAR** THINGS...

Snap

TO **SEE** THINGS...

AND IF YOU STOOD, BARELY BREATHING, AS NIGHT CREPT UPON THE FOREST, YOU WOULD BEGIN TO **FEEL** SOMETHING TOO-- SOMETHING **MAGICAL**!

FOR THE FOREST OF BURZEE IS NO ORDINARY FOREST. THERE IS A REASON IT HAS GROWN SO PROUDLY FOR SO LONG.

IT HAS **CARETAKERS**...

1

TO TEND AND NURTURE THE TREES, TO PROTECT THE FOREST FROM FLAME AND BLADE, AND TO RESIST THE DEADLY ADVANCE OF MORTAL CIVILIZATION; OTHERWISE WE INVITE DESTRUCTION.

FOR YEARS, DAUGHTER OF THE FOREST, YOU HAVE FOLLOWED THE LAW. IN PRACTICING YOUR TASKS WITH JOY AND LOVING CARE YOU HAVE GROWN DEAR TO MY HEART.

BUT THREE DAYS AGO WHILE TENDING A YOUNG NISK TREE AT THE FOREST'S EDGE, YOU PERFORMED A *FORBIDDEN* ACT -- YOU LET A MORTAL MAN STEAL A *KISS.* KNOWING MY MAGIC WOULD DETECT THIS ACT, YOU NEVERTHELESS TRIED TO KEEP IT SECRET. DO I SPEAK TRULY?

Y-YOUR MAJESTY, I --

DO I SPEAK *TRULY* ?

-- I --

...YES, YOUR MAJESTY.

OH, NELANTHE... MY HEART FADES BLACK WITH GRIEF, BUT MY DUTY TO THE LAW REMAINS CLEAR. YOU ARE NO LONGER A DAUGHTER OF THE FOREST. I REVOKE YOUR IMMORTALITY AND *BANISH* YOU FROM BURZEE FOREVER.

NO, YOUR MAJESTY! IF YOU TAKE AWAY HER IMMORTALITY, SHE'LL GROW OLD AND DIE LIKE -- LIKE -- A *MORTAL!*

SILENCE, NEBELLE, BEFORE I BANISH YOU, TOO! THE LAW OF THE FOREST MUST BE UPHELD!

GO, NELANTHE, YOU ARE A MORTAL NOW. RUN AND JOIN YOUR KIND! RUN, NELANTHE, *RUN, RUN...*

3

...RUN...

So NELANTHE RUNS, LEAVING BEHIND ALL THAT SHE LOVES...

LEAVING BEHIND THE LIFE SHE WAS MEANT TO LIVE...

KNOWING THAT DEATH, CONSTANTLY HOVERING NEAR, WILL SOONER OR LATER STRIKE.

≥GASP≤

≥GASP≤

≥CHOKE≤

WHO ARE YOU?!

DON'T BE AFRAID. I'M MERELY THE KING OF THE TROLLS, OUT FOR A MOONLIGHT STROLL. PLEASE... WHY DO YOU SPOIL YOUR LOVELI-NESS WITH TEARS, LITTLE WOOD-NYMPH?

WHAT IS YOUR TROUBLE, PRETTY ONE?

4

I--I'M NOT A WOOD-NYMPH ANYMORE. I BROKE THE LAW OF THE FOREST, SO THEY BANISHED ME FROM BURZEE.

NOW I'M JUST A MORTAL, YOUR MAJESTY.

WHAT? SURELY NO ONE AS *BEAUTIFUL* AS YOU COULD DESERVE SUCH JUDGMENT. THE PUNISHMENT IS FAR TOO *CRUEL*!

I...DON'T KNOW...

WELL, *I* KNOW... I KNOW YOU'RE MORE BEAUTIFUL THAN ANYTHING ON EARTH, ABOVE, OR BENEATH IT. ONLY THE WOOD-NYMPH QUEEN CAN RESTORE YOUR IMMORTALITY, BUT *I* CAN GIVE YOU LUXURY A WOOD-NYMPH NEVER DREAMS OF! I'LL MAKE YOU MY *QUEEN*. COME WITH ME--I'LL GIVE YOU GOLD AND JEWELS, GORGEOUS CLOTHING, SERVANTS--WHATEVER YOU DESIRE YOU WILL HAVE!

--BUT--

THERE LIES MY KINGDOM--THAT EXTINCT VOLCANO. DARK AND UGLY ON THE OUTSIDE--YET, OH, WHAT WONDERS AWAIT *INSIDE*! COME, BE MY QUEEN! WHERE ELSE HAVE YOU TO GO?

...NOWHERE...

ALL RIGHT, *YES*, I'LL COME WITH YOU!

*T*HREE HOURS LATER, DEEP WITHIN THE DEAD VOLCANO...

...AND WITH THIS CUP I TAKE YOU AS ROYAL CONSORT, PRONOUNCING YOU QUEEN OF THE TROLLS FOREVER.

5

THE TROLL KING'S PROMISES ALL COME TRUE -- BUT, AS THE MONTHS PASS, NELANTHE BROODS.

THE KING IS RIGHT. TAKING AWAY MY IMMORTALITY WASN'T JUSTICE -- IT WAS *CRUELTY!* I KISSED A MORTAL MAN -- *ONCE* -- SO WHAT? I ONLY WANTED TO KNOW WHAT IT WAS LIKE. *HE* DID MOST OF THE KISSING ANYWAY -- NOT ME.

BUT THOSE STUPID WOOD-NYMPHS WOULDN'T LISTEN. THEY WERE *JEALOUS* -- YES, THAT'S IT. WELL, IF THEY SAW ME NOW, I'D SHOW THEM *REASON* TO BE JEALOUS! AND THAT PUSHY, SMIRKING ZURLINE -- HOW I *HATE* HER AND HER SILLY LAW OF THE FOREST. THE FOREST HAS LIVED FOR CENTURIES. IT WILL *GO ON* LIVING -- UNLESS..

I MUST SUMMON A COUNCIL IMMEDIATELY!

YOUR MAJESTY, HONORED COUNCILLORS, I HAVE CALLED YOU TONIGHT BECAUSE I WISH TO PROPOSE AN *IDEA,* ONE I URGENTLY HOPE YOU'LL SUPPORT.

TELL US YOUR PROPOSAL.

BY MAKING ME MORTAL, THE WOOD-NYMPHS GAVE ME THE GIFT OF *DEATH.* NOW I BURN TO RETURN IT TO THEM.

I PROPOSE *WAR* -- COMPLETE WAR UPON THE FOREST OF BURZEE UNTIL NEITHER TWIG STANDS NOR SEED SPROUTS!

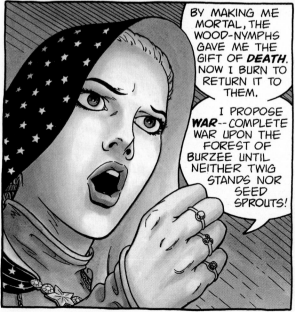

YOUR HIGHNESS, THE WOOD-NYMPHS ARE OUR NATURAL *ENEMIES.* WE'VE LONG DESIRED TO DESTROY THEM, BUT THE CHANCE OF SUCCESS IS SO SLIGHT THAT--

HEH HEH...

THAT'S RIGHT, ≋SNORT≋ OUR TROLL ARMY COULD NEVER DEFEAT THEIR *MAGIC.*

REMEMBER THAT I WAS ONCE A WOOD-NYMPH; I KNOW THEIR WEAKNESSES. FIRST WE MUST STRIKE THE FOREST BEFORE THE WOOD-NYMPHS REALIZE WHAT WE ARE DOING. OUR ARMY MUST ATTACK AT *NIGHT*, SECRETLY--OTHERWISE THEY WILL EASILY STOP US.

SECONDLY, *FIRE* IS THE QUICKEST AND MOST DEADLY WAY TO DESTROY THE FOREST. WE MUST ENLIST AS OUR ALLIES THE FIRE-BREATHING DRAGONS FROM THE LAVA PITS FAR BELOW THIS VOLCANO. WITH SURPRISE AND THE DRAGONS ON OUR SIDE WE WILL SUCCEED.

THE *DRAGONS?!* ≶SNORT≷ *THEY* CAN'T BE TRUSTED.

NEITHER CAN *WE*--AND THEY HATE THE WOOD-NYMPHS AS MUCH AS WE DO--PERHAPS *MORE*.

CONSIDER, TOO, YOUR MAJESTY--HEH HEH--YOU'VE TOLERATED THE DRAGON'S INDEPENDENCE LONG ENOUGH. THIS COULD BE THE FIRST STEP IN--HEH HEH--BRINGING THEM UNDER *YOUR* POWER!

YES. THE DESTRUCTION OF BURZEE--A GOAL I'VE LONG HOPED TO REACH. AND SUDDENLY, THE GOAL'S WITHIN MY *GRASP!*

THEN YOU DECLARE WAR?

YES, MY QUEEN... I DECLARE WAR.

HEH HEH...

THE KING CONTACTS THE DRAGONS, THE TROLLS SHARPEN THEIR AXES, THE ARMY DRILLS--ALL IN PREPARATION FOR THE NIGHT OF THE NEXT *FULL MOON*--THE NIGHT OF THE *ATTACK!*

7

THE NIGHT ARRIVES.

OH, WHAT'S THE MATTER WITH ME? EVER SINCE THE KING DECLARED WAR, I'VE BEEN HAVING SECOND THOUGHTS.

WHY?

WHY?

SOMETIMES I ALMOST WISH TO *RETURN* TO BURZEE... TO LAUGH WITH THE OTHERS BY CRYSTAL SPRINGS...

...TO DANCE UPON THE SUNBEAMS THAT SPLIT THE LAYERS OF GLOWING LEAVES... AND, AH, TO TEND THE MAGNIFICENT *TREES*...

THE *CURSED* TREES! SLAVING OVER THEM DAY AFTER DAY-- AND FOR WHAT? USELESS, *USELESS*, *USELESS*!

rrrip

YAAAA!

CRASH

IF ONLY I COULD *FORGET*! I *NEED* TO FORGET! BUT HOW?

HOW? I CAN'T GO-- OH!

WHAT'S THIS?

ENCYCLOPÆDIA of MAGIC
The Water of Oblivion.
In the royal gardens of the Emerald City is the forbidden Fountain containing the potent Water of Oblivion. This water is capable of completely erasing the memory of any being who drinks it. For this reason Ozma, ruler of Oz, has decreed the water forbidden to all.
Long ago Glinda, Good Sorceress of the South, placed the fountain in 1043

...nd of A-Ramose
...owerful spell.
...f Velkemin
...lden Valley of
Sea of Sighs
...race of wasps
...agical stings.
...sting of a wasp
...painful, though
...granted to the
the stinger is
e wasp dies.

THE FULL MOON SHINES OVER THE EMERALD CITY OF OZ AND INTO THE PALACE BEDROOM OF DOROTHY GALE.

WURF?

WHAT'S THE MATTER, TOTO? GO BACK TO SLEEP.

WOOF

WHAT IS IT, TOTO? IS SOMEONE ON THE TERRACE?

SCRITCH SCRATCH

I DON'T SEE ANYONE.

WOOF WOOF

SHH, YOU'LL WAKE THE WHOLE -- WHOOPS!

STILL A LITTLE SLIPPERY FROM THE RAIN THIS AFTERNOON.

WOOF

GRRR...

TOTO, WHAT DO YOU *HEAR*?

WOOF WOOF WOOF

SCHH

TOTO!

OH, NO!

TOTO! TOTO!

10

I HOPE YOU ENJOY MY SONGS, FRIEND SAWHORSE. I'M AFRAID THAT AT NICK CHOPPER'S THEY FALL ON TIN EARS.

IT'S ALL VERY WELL TO PRAISE YOUR OWN BRAINS--BUT HOW DO YOU KNOW THEY'RE SO SUPERIOR?

WELL, I'M RIDING--YOU'RE THE ONE WALKING...

HELP

HELP

QUIET FOR A SECOND!

HEAR WHAT?

DO YOU HEAR THAT?

HELP

YOU NEED THE PAINT ON YOUR EARS TOUCHED UP.

LOOK UP THERE!

A GIANT BAT-- AND IT'S GOT DOROTHY!

HELP

AT LEAST YOUR EYES HAVEN'T FLAKED OFF! IT IS DOROTHY, AND SHE'S IN TROUBLE-- HOLD ON!

YAWP!

12

OVER THE FERTILE FIELDS OF OZ FLASH THE TIRELESS LEGS OF THE SAWHORSE.

MU-MU-MUST YOU RU-RUN S-SO BU-BU-*BUMPILY*?

CAN'T HELP IT--BESIDES, NO ONE ELSE IN OZ COULD KEEP UP WITH THAT BAT.

KEEP YOUR EYE ON IT. WE CAN'T AFFORD TO LOSE IT BEFORE IT LANDS!

BU-BUT WHAT I-IF IT FLIES O-O-OVER THE...

...*DESERT*?

WHAT NOW?

DOROTHY NEEDS HELP-- *LET'S GO!*

DANGER! TURN BACK!
YOU HAVE REACHED THE
DEADLY DESERT
WHICH COMPLETELY SURROUNDS THE
MARVELOUS LAND *of* OZ.
ONE TOUCH OF THESE DANGEROUS
SANDS WILL TURN ANY LIVING
FLESH TO DUST IN AN INSTANT.
ALL PERSONS ARE WARNED TO
STAND WELL AWAY FROM THE EDGE
TO AVOID BEING OVERCOME BY
DESERT'S NOXIOUS FUMES.

BUT--

LOOK, *I'M* NOT MADE OF FLESH, AND MY FEET ARE SHOD WITH GOLD AS WELL. IF *YOU'RE* SCARED, JUST DON'T FALL OFF.

BUT THE *NOXIOUS FUMES*--!

YOU'RE STUFFED WITH *STRAW!* YOU DON'T BREATHE AND NEITHER DO I -- STOP WORRYING!

YOU'RE RIGHT.

I WONDER WHY MY BRAINS NEVER THOUGHT OF THIS BEFORE...

QUICK, NIGHTSHADE, DID YOU GET IT?

YES, YOUR HIGHNESS.

AHHH! PERFECT, YOU'VE SERVED ME WELL!

...OOOHH...

...OHHH... MY ARMS...

≥PANT≥ ≥PANT≥

NIGHTSHADE, *WHAT* ARE *THOSE*?

I DON'T KNOW, YOUR HIGHNESS. THEY GRABBED ONTO ME IN THE EMERALD CITY, BUT YOU TOLD ME TO STOP FOR NOTHING, SO I IGNORED THEM.

YOU *SHOULD* HAVE DROPPED THEM OVER THE DESERT-- BUT NEVER MIND.

SWEEP THEM INTO THE CRATER AND WE NEEDN'T THINK OF IT AGAIN.

...OZ-OZMA WILL FIND OUT...

OZMA! WHY WOULD *SHE* BE INTERESTED?

15

16

YOU'RE NO TROLL!

WHAT ARE YOU?

I AM... THE QUEEN...

OF THE TROLLS...

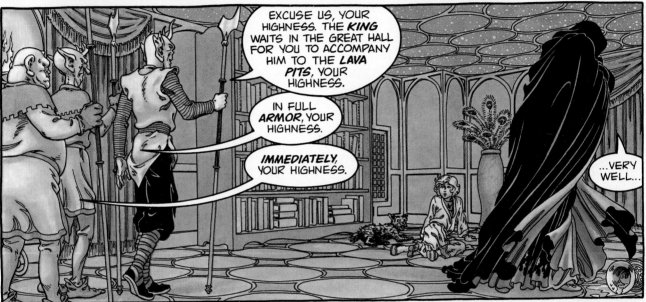

EXCUSE US, YOUR HIGHNESS. THE KING WAITS IN THE GREAT HALL FOR YOU TO ACCOMPANY HIM TO THE LAVA PITS, YOUR HIGHNESS.

IN FULL ARMOR, YOUR HIGHNESS.

IMMEDIATELY, YOUR HIGHNESS.

...VERY WELL...

ONE OF YOU, GO TO THE KING, TELL HIM I FOLLOW SHORTLY--THEN RETURN TO HELP ME WITH MY ARMOR.

YOU OTHERS, REMAIN HERE TO GUARD THESE PRISONERS.

DON'T HURT THEM...

CLICK

...BUT BE CERTAIN NOT TO LET THEM ESCAPE.

I MUST DRESS QUICKLY.

19

...BRAINS...

GRRRIINDD..

OH, NO! THE BOULDER--

CAREFUL OF MY--

FLUMP

--IT'S ROLLING *BACK!*

WE'LL BE *TRAPPED!*

..RRRIINDD..

UGH! I CAN'T BUDGE IT! IT'S TOO HEAVY!

KEEP TRYING! IT MOVED SO EASILY BEFORE!

HEY! WHERE'S THAT *LIGHT* COMING FROM?

WHAT?

WE'RE IN A *TUNNEL!* WE'RE *NOT* TRAPPED!

COME ON. LET'S FIND OUT FOR SURE.

I JUST HOPE WE DON'T MEET ANY GIANT BATS WAITING TO SWOOP DOWN ON OUR HEADS.

SHORTLY.

SOMEONE MUST **LIVE** HERE.

I GUESS WE STUMBLED THROUGH THEIR **BACK DOOR.**

LOOK--**MORE** PASSAGES!

I WONDER IF DOROTHY'S AROUND HERE SOMEWHERE.

MAYBE WE CAN DISCOVER SOMETHING UP AHEAD.

BACK! BACK!

WHAT? WHAT?

SHHH...

WHAT'S TAKING THE QUEEN SO LONG? SHE KNOWS WE HAVE TO SUMMON THE DRAGONS. IF WE MAKE THEM WAIT MUCH LONGER, THEY'LL WITHDRAW FROM THE ATTACK! ONE OF YOU, GO TO HER APARTMENT AND--

NO NEED, YOUR MAJESTY.

HERE I AM.

YOU'RE LATE!

FORGIVE ME, YOUR MAJESTY.

COME QUICKLY! DAWN DRAWS EVER NEARER, AND WE CANNOT SECRETLY ATTACK BURZEE *AFTER* SUNRISE.

THEY'RE COMING THIS WAY!

I WAS UNFORSEEABLY DELAYED.

HOW STRANGE THAT *TONIGHT* YOU MEET DELAY. YOU'RE NOT HAVING SECOND THOUGHTS I HOPE.

SECOND THOUGHTS, YOUR MAJESTY? NOT *I*!

AT THIS MOMENT MY CONSUMING NEED IS TO *DESTROY* THAT FOREST AND WIPE THE WOODNYMPHS FROM MY MEMORY *FOREVER*!

HA-*HA*! VERY GOOD!

ON TO THE *LAVA PITS*!

ARE THEY GONE?

YES, THEY TURNED DOWN ANOTHER HALLWAY.

AWP! WHAT'S THAT?

WOOOSH-SH

23

24

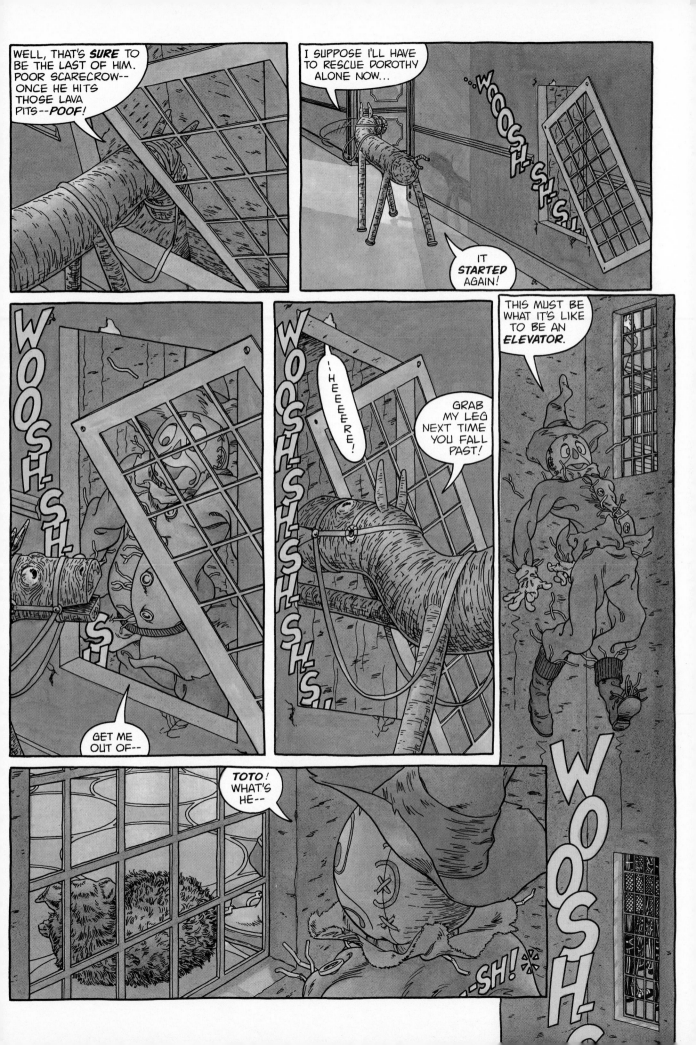

--DOING HERE?

TOTO! *WAKE UP!*

SCARECROW!

DORO-- SHH!

?

BE QUIET--TWO TROLL GUARDS.

HOW'D YOU GET IN THERE?

NEVER MIND NOW. THE SAWHORSE IS WITH ME-- HOW DO WE *RESCUE* YOU?

I DON'T KNOW. WE'RE PRISONERS IN THE TROLL QUEEN'S APARTMENT.

OH, *HER!* I THINK WE CAN FIND YOU!

BE CAREFUL! DON'T LET THE TROLLS CATCH YOU!

DON'T WORRY-- THEY'RE TOO BUSY PREPARING A SECRET ATTACK ON BURZEEEEEEEEEE...

WHAT'S HAPPENED TO HIM? THE AIR CURRENT STOPPED AWHI--

SPLOP

WHO'RE YOU *TALKING* TO?

UH--MY *DOG*--

WELL, *DON'T!*

BURZEE...? ISN'T THAT THE HUGE, OLD FOREST FULL OF MAGICAL BEINGS I'VE HEARD OZMA TALK ABOUT? IF THE TROLLS ARE GOING TO *ATTACK* THE FOREST...

DOROTHY! TOTO!

HUNH?

YII!

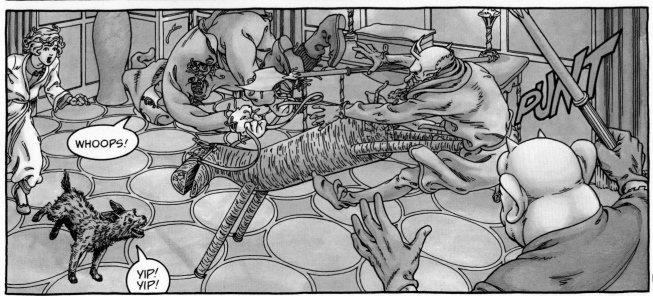

WHOOPS!

PUNT

YIP! YIP!

27

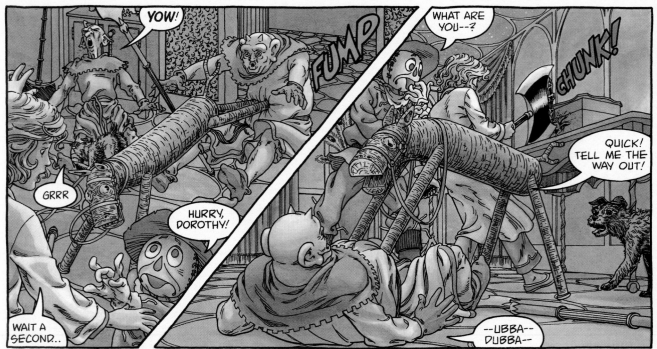

TELL ME. ...O-OZ PEOPLE-- I DIDN'T--

OZ?! WHAT HAVE YOU DONE? IF OZMA KNOWS ABOUT THIS...! ARE YOU TRYING TO RUIN ALL MY PLANS--PLANS I'VE NURTURED SINCE THE DAY YOU KISSED ME AT THE EDGE OF THE FOREST!?!

FOR YEARS I'VE BEEN TRYING TO LEARN THE WOOD-NYMPHS' SECRETS! WHO BETTER TO LEARN THEM FROM THAN A WOOD-NYMPH? LISTEN TO ME, MY QUEEN--I, DISGUISED BY MAGIC! I WAS THAT MORTAL MAN!

WHAT...WHAT DO YOU MEAN...?

YOU HAVEN'T GUESSED? DO YOU THINK THAT WHAT'S HAPPENED TO YOU HAS BEEN BY CHANCE?

YOU--? THEN IT'S YOUR FAULT-- MY BANISHMENT-- MY MORTALITY--ALL BECAUSE OF YOU!

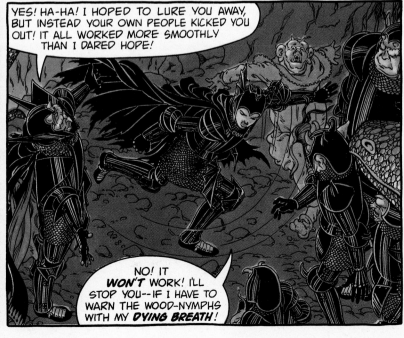

YES! HA-HA! I HOPED TO LURE YOU AWAY, BUT INSTEAD YOUR OWN PEOPLE KICKED YOU OUT! IT ALL WORKED MORE SMOOTHLY THAN I DARED HOPE!

NO! IT WON'T WORK! I'LL STOP YOU--IF I HAVE TO WARN THE WOOD-NYMPHS WITH MY DYING BREATH!

31

STOP HER!

YOU REALLY SHOULD HAVE LET ME BURN HER....

FORGET HER-- MY OFFICERS WILL TAKE CARE OF HER. ALL THAT MATTERS NOW IS THAT WE DESTROY THE FOREST. WE MARCH AT ONCE!

VERY GOOD. IF I DON'T BURN SOMETHING SOON I'LL EXPLODE!

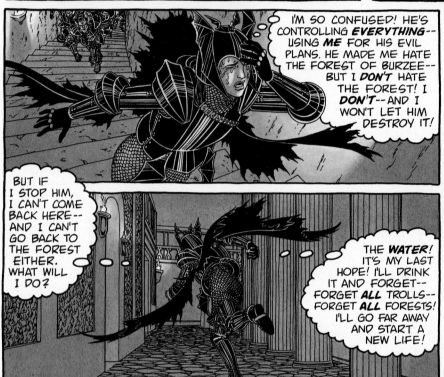

I'M SO CONFUSED! HE'S CONTROLLING *EVERYTHING*-- USING *ME* FOR HIS EVIL PLANS. HE MADE ME HATE THE FOREST OF BURZEE-- BUT I *DON'T* HATE THE FOREST! I *DON'T*--AND I WON'T LET HIM DESTROY IT!

THE WATER! AT LEAST I HAVE THE WA--

NO!!

BUT IF I STOP HIM, I CAN'T COME BACK HERE-- AND I CAN'T GO BACK TO THE FOREST EITHER. WHAT WILL I DO?

THE *WATER!* IT'S MY LAST HOPE! I'LL DRINK IT AND FORGET-- FORGET *ALL* TROLLS-- FORGET *ALL* FORESTS! I'LL GO FAR AWAY AND START A NEW LIFE!

STOP HER!

THAT *DOROTHY* TOOK IT! WELL, SHE COULDN'T HAVE RUN FAR. CAN'T SHE UNDERSTAND HOW MUCH I NEED IT? WITHOUT IT MY LIFE'S OVER!

ARE THEY FOLLOWING US?

I DON'T SEE ANY--

YOW! IT'S THE *GIANT BAT!*

HURRY, SAWHORSE -- THE FOREST CAN'T BE TOO FAR. I SAW IT WHEN THE BAT CARRIED ME HERE.

I THINK IT'S *GAINING* ON US!

THERE'S A *DROP-OFF* AHEAD!

HOLD ON!

YOWCH!

plumf

CLOP

WAIT!

WOOF WOOF WOOF

34

35

...GROANNN...

--OH, WHY?... WHY?

THE FOREST...THE FOREST...HOW I LOVED YOU. I *STILL* L-LOVE YOU--! B-BUT I R-RUINED E-EVERYTH-THING... I WISH I W-WAS *D-DEAD*!

OH! THE ARMY-- ALREADY SO *CLOSE*!

THERE'S NO TIME TO WARN THE WOOD-NYMPHS--THEY WOULDN'T LISTEN TO ME ANYWAY! I HAVE TO STOP THE ARMY MYSELF-- *SOMEHOW*!

THE FOREST *MUST* BE PROTECTED-- EVEN IF I'M THE ONE WHO HAS TO DO IT.

UP, NIGHT-SHADE! FLY! *QUICK-LY*!

SQUEE?

FLAP FLUTTER FLOP

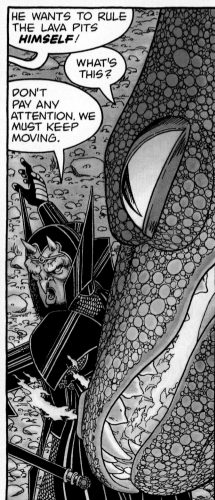

HE'S *LURING* YOU TO BURZEE TO BE *DESTROYED* BY THE WOOD-NYMPHS!

THAT'S NON-SENSE!

THE WOOD-NYMPHS DO HAVE POWERFUL MAGIC, DON'T THEY?

I MAY BE MISTAKEN-- YOU ALL LOOK THE SAME TO ME-- BUT ISN'T THAT THE QUEEN OF THE TROLLS?

YES--SHE *WAS.* BUT SHE'S GONE CRAZY! *YOU* HEARD HER BACK IN THE CAVERN.

KEEP *ON*--DAWN'S NOT FAR OFF.

WAIT A MOMENT, YOU SEEM A LITTLE TOO *EAGER*...

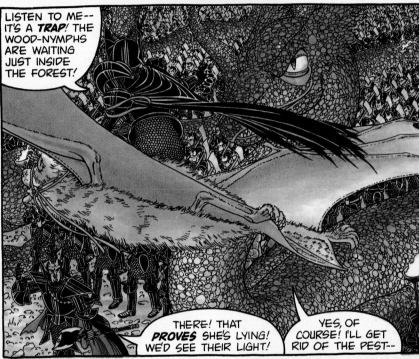

LISTEN TO ME-- IT'S A *TRAP!* THE WOOD-NYMPHS ARE WAITING JUST INSIDE THE FOREST!

THERE! THAT *PROVES* SHE'S LYING! WE'D SEE THEIR LIGHT!

YES, OF COURSE! I'LL GET RID OF THE PEST--

FWOOOSH!

SQUEEE-

OH, NIGHT-SHADE, NIGHT-SHADE, WHAT CAN I DO? THEY'RE STILL ADVANCING.

39

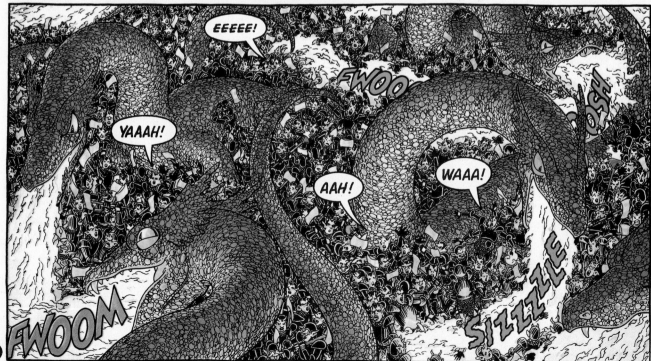

40

THAT WAS EASY--ONE LOOK AND THEY ALL FLED.

I'D HAVE THOUGHT THEY'D PUT UP MORE OF A FIGHT.

NEVERTHELESS, I MUST THANK YOU, PRINCESS DOROTHY, AND YOU TOO, SAW-HORSE, FOR WARNING US. IF THE TROLLS HAD MANAGED TO SURPRISE US--

EEEK!

AWAY, NIGHT-SHADE!

THE TROLL QUEEN!

SHE HAS THE WATER!

QUICK, MY NYMPHS-- THE BRANCHES!

SQUEEEE!

FLY, NIGHT-SHADE! *FLY!*

SNAP

CRACK

CRACKLE

SNAP

RRRRRRR

THUD

LOOK WHO IT IS--

--NELANTHE!

UHHH...

NELANTHE, YOU'RE HURT! DON'T MOVE--

≈COUGH≈ L-LEAVE ME ALONE! YOU TOOK THE FOREST AWAY FROM ME! ≈COUGH≈ ≈COUGH≈

YOU *KNOW* THE TROLL QUEEN?

YES, ONCE SHE WAS ONE OF US. HOW SHE FELL IN WITH THE TROLLS I DON'T KNOW.

YOUR MAJESTY, HELP HER! I THINK SHE'S *DYING!*

THE WATER...

THE ONLY WAY I CAN HELP IS TO RESTORE HER IMMORTALITY.

THEN DO IT!

BUT THE LAW OF THE FOREST...

WOOF WOOF

SCARECROW! TOTO!

DOROTHY! SAWHORSE! YOU'RE SAFE!

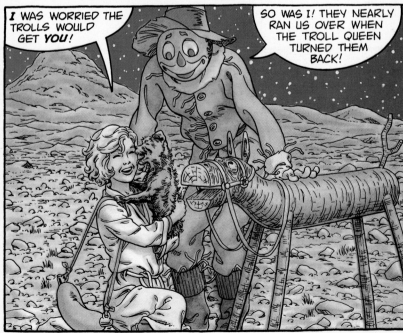

I WAS WORRIED THE TROLLS WOULD GET *YOU!*

SO WAS *I!* THEY NEARLY RAN US OVER WHEN THE TROLL QUEEN TURNED THEM BACK!

TROLL QUEEN? YOU MUST MEAN THE **WOOD-NYMPH** QUEEN.

NO, THE **TROLL** QUEEN TRICKED THE DRAGONS INTO ATTACKING THE TROLLS...

WHAT?

BUT THAT MEANS SHE TURNED AGAINST THE TROLLS TO SAVE THE FOREST! THEN SHE HAS **NOTHING LEFT** --EXCEPT...

...EXCEPT THE WATER OF OBLIVION.

BUT I--I **CAN'T** GIVE IT TO HER. OZMA'S FORBIDDEN IT.

CAN IT HELP HER?

I DON'T KNOW, BUT--

AHHHHHHHHH

OH, **SO WHAT** IF IT'S FORBIDDEN. I'LL BE IN DEEP TROUBLE WHEN I GET BACK TO THE EMERALD CITY, BUT I DON'T CARE ANYMORE.

POP

PLEASE DRINK IT. YOU WANTED IT SO DESPERATELY.

NO!

I--I DON'T WANT IT ANYMORE ≩COUGH≩ ≩COUGH≩ --ALL I WANT IS THE FOREST--ALL I *EVER* WANTED--ALL I *EVER* LOVED! BUT THEY TOOK IT AWAY, SO I TRIED TO FORGET--BUT I *CAN'T*--I *CAN'T!* AHRGH!

THE FOREST-- THE FOREST-- ≩COUGH COUGH≩ --UHHHHHHHH....

THIS IS TOO MUCH--I CANNOT ABANDON HER. I'M GOING TO RESTORE HER IMMORTALITY.

YOUR MAJES-TY--!

THE LAW OF THE FOREST!

HOW CAN YOU--?

SILENCE!

WHEN I BANISHED NELANTHE MY HEART GRIEVED, BUT HER HEART IS *BREAKING*. IF SHE DIES NOW MY HEART WILL BREAK ALSO.

SHE LOVES THE FOREST DEEPLY. SURELY HER TURNING THE TROLL ARMY BACK PROVES THAT. I RESPECT THE LAW, BUT THE LAW CANNOT SEE A BROKEN HEART. NELANTHE *BELONGS* IN BURZEE-- THAT IS MOST IMPORTANT NOW.

OH, *HURRY*, YOUR MAJESTY--!

45

NELANTHE, YOU **ARE** IMMORTAL--

YOU **ARE** A DAUGHTER OF THE FOREST!

OH...

OH, YOUR MAJESTY! IS IT TRUE? THANK YOU! THANK YOU! FORGIVE ME FOR BREAKING THE LAW.

RISE, NELANTHE. I'M THE ONE WHO NEEDS FORGIVENESS. I DIDN'T REALIZE HOW MUCH YOU LOVE THE FOREST-- PERHAPS NOW YOU LOVE IT MORE THAN I.

WELCOME BACK TO BURZEE, NELANTHE.

OH, YES, NEBELLE-- BURZEE! I CAN HARDLY BELIEVE IT--BUT IT'S **TRUE!** IT'S **TRUE!**

ERIC SHANOWER 1988

46

The End